This book belongs to:

_ _

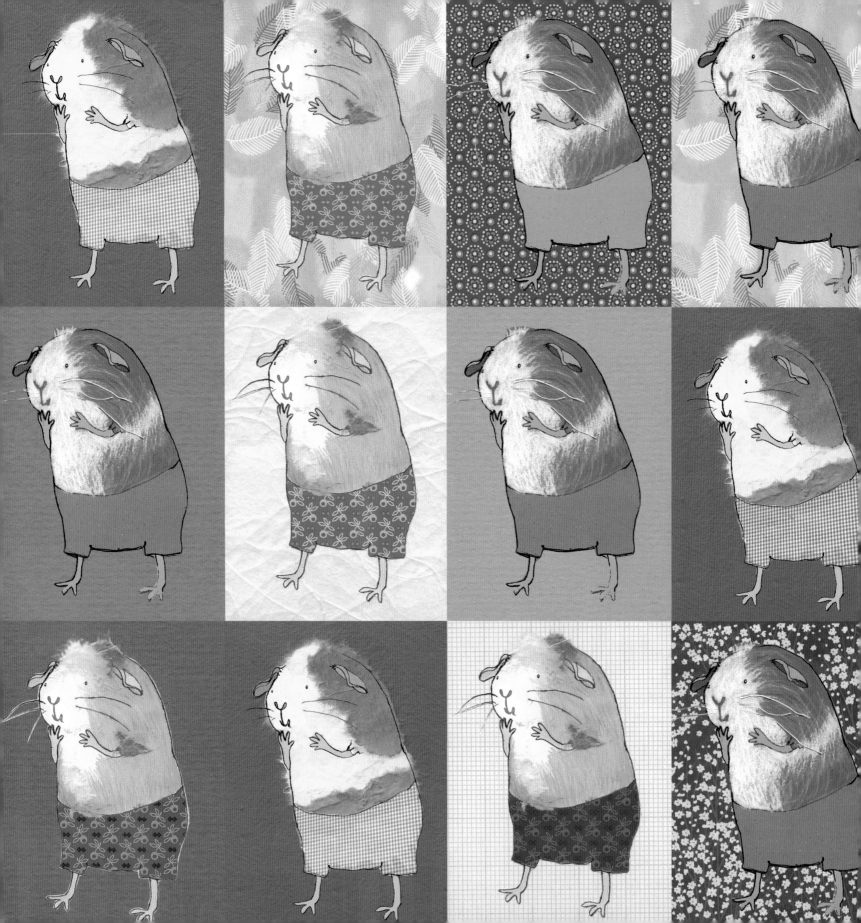

For Betty and Jack, with fond memories.

Nicola and Charlotte

OXFORD
UNIVERSITY PRESS

Great Clarendon Street, Oxford OX2 6DP

Oxford University Press is a department of the University of Oxford.
It furthers the University's objective of excellence in research, scholarship,
and education by publishing worldwide in

Oxford   New York

Auckland Cape Town Dar es Salaam Hong Kong Karachi
Kuala Lumpur Madrid Melbourne Mexico City Nairobi
New Delhi Shanghai Taipei Toronto

With offices in

Argentina Austria Brazil Chile Czech Republic France Greece
Guatemala Hungary Italy Japan Poland Portugal Singapore
South Korea Switzerland Thailand Turkey Ukraine Vietnam

Oxford is a registered trade mark of Oxford University Press
in the UK and in certain other countries

British Library Cataloguing in Publication Data available

ISBN: 978-0-19-273997-1

2 4 6 8 10 9 7 5 3 1

Printed in China

Paper used in the production of this book is a natural,
recyclable product made from wood grown in sustainable forests.
The manufacturing process conforms to the environmental
regulations of the country of origin

CHARLOTTE MIDDLETON
presents

CHRISTOPHER Nibble

in a tale of dandelion derring-do!

OXFORD
UNIVERSITY PRESS

If there was one thing Christopher Nibble **loved** more than football,

it was . . .

eating dandelion leaves.

He ate
dandelion leaves...

at breakfast
time,

at lunch
time,

and at
dinner time.

And if Christopher felt
peckish between meals,
he ate...

MORE dandelion leaves!
But it was not just Christopher who liked
dandelion leaves. Mr and Mrs Nibble liked them.
His sister liked them. His friends liked them.

In fact. . . every guinea pig
in Dandeville **loved** dandelion leaves.

munch

munch

nibble

munch

nibble

All day long the happy
sound of munching and
nibbling filled the air. . .

until, that is,
dandelion leaves
began to
run out.

Dandelion dishes
were taken off
the menus, and
dandelion drinks
disappeared from
the shelves.

Menu Today

Carrot and lettuce wrap on
a bed of ~~dandelion leaves~~
cabbage

~~Dandelion~~ soup
cabbage

cabbage
~~Dandelion~~ and
broccoli quiche

~~Dandelion~~
juice sold out

The last few leaves could be bought
on the internet . . .

for a HUGE amount of money!

Soon the worst thing imaginable happened. . .

all over town the dandelions had been
munched to nothing more than bitten-down
stalks, and the guinea pigs had to make do. . .

with chewy cabbage instead!

Just one dandelion was left but nobody knew about it, except Christopher Nibble. It happened to be growing right outside his bedroom window.

Christopher's mouth
watered at the sight of it.

But he knew he mustn't eat it,
or let anyone else eat it,
not if it was the last dandelion in town.

It might even be the last dandelion
in the whole world!
He thought hard and decided. . .

... to go to the library.

Cookery

MONTY POIS
The Oriental Cabbage
NIBBLE'S CHRISTMAS
DAN DE LEON
PRIDE & POISSON
GORDON RHUBARB
101 Lettuce Recipes
Hollyhock Magic!
THE VERY HUNGRY GRUB
JAMIE CAULIFLOWER
CHEESE PLEASE
Pippi Parsnip
Ready, Steady, Nibble
WAR @ PIZZA

Sports

The Tour de Dandeville
MINI GOLF
MARATHON MOUSE
FOOTBALL MAD
SOCCER
CYCLING FOR GERBILS

Flowers

Dandelions

Weeds

Cloche Gardening
Shoots, Leaves & Weeds
The LAWN EATING EXPERT
Brassica Breeding

THE N A O WEEDS

THE VERY HUNGRY GUINEA PIG

Bugs

QUIET PLEASE!

He borrowed a book called 'Everything You Need to Know about Dandelions'

and he read it very carefully.

He found a little cloche to protect his dandelion. . .

and every day he watered it and picked off the bugs.

Every day he was very
good about not taking
even the tiniest
little nibble
while he . . .

waited,
and waited,
and waited.

Until, finally, his dandelion had grown the most beautiful white head of tiny seeds.

Very gently,
Christopher picked it
and carried it all
the way up
Daisy Chain Hill.
When he reached
the top. . .

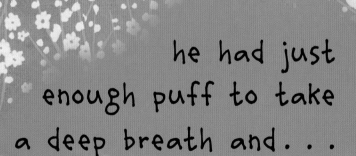

he had just
enough puff to take
a deep breath and. . .

The seeds filled the air...

and landed gently all over Dandeville.

At first nobody noticed.

But soon the new
plants started to sprout
fresh leaves.

And in no time at all Dandeville
was filled with the happy sound
of munching once more.

As for Christopher,

But now

there's

something

he loves just

as much

as eating

dandelions. . . .

Christopher loves **GROWING** them!

Picture books from Oxford are perfect for sharing...

PIGEON PIE
OH MY!

Feathers will fly in this funny farmyard drama!

Written by
DEBBIE SINGLETON

Illustrated by
KRISTYNA LITTEN

978-0-19-273415-0 (pb)

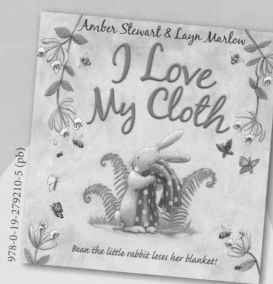

Amber Stewart & Layn Marlow

I Love My Cloth

Bean the little rabbit loses her blanket!

978-0-19-279210-5 (pb)

The really, really, really big dinosaur

Richard Byrne

978-0-19-275764-7 (pb)

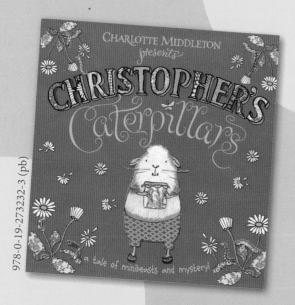

CHARLOTTE MIDDLETON presents

CHRISTOPHER'S Caterpillars

a tale of minibeasts and mystery!

978-0-19-273232-3 (pb)

Ann Bonwill • Simon Rickerty

I don't want to be a pea!

featuring Hugo and Bella

978-0-19-278018-8 (pb)

Available in all good bookshops or online at www.oxfordchildrens.co.uk